Leaves of Grass
Revisited,
Short Stories,
and
Reflections in Poetry

Richard Dean Holmberg

ISBN 979-8-89345-358-4 (paperback)
ISBN 979-8-89345-359-1 (digital)

Copyright © 2024 by Richard Dean Holmberg

All rights reserved. No part of this publication may be reproduced, distributed, or transmitted in any form or by any means, including photocopying, recording, or other electronic or mechanical methods without the prior written permission of the publisher. For permission requests, solicit the publisher via the address below.

Christian Faith Publishing
832 Park Avenue
Meadville, PA 16335
www.christianfaithpublishing.com

Printed in the United States of America

To Holly, the best decision of my life.

Introduction

My name is Richard, and recently my life and career have taken a turn into some dark passages. When I was a young man, my father gave me a book: *How to Win Friends and Influence People*. The book offered a road map for a successful life and career. Unfortunately, it turned out to be the wrong road for me, as time will show.

My early efforts in twenty years of personnel and employee relations were surprisingly successful. My natural empathy served me well in identifying and counseling those who needed it. As the years passed, I was given promotions and added responsibilities until I was in "over my head," with tasks beyond my skills and training (i.e., payroll, benefits, and work measurement). Then came the '80s, and my job changed from employee relations to "change agent." The bean counters took over, and instead of goals, all we had was P/L and head counts. The benefits of umbrellas started to spring leaks. The old *work-for-life* contracts were nullified or limited. The environment in the office was more frightening and political. We were all friendly casualties in a war of change. The Information Age was upon us. Computers were smaller, faster, and their influence larger, eventually dominating the office. We became only end users.

Do you remember the old Laurel and Hardy movie where Stan was left guarding an old bunker many years after the war had ended? He sat on top of a mountain of tin rations consumed. We are like Stan. We are sentries guarding a fort of values long since moved. Like Stan, we believe in our duty with heart and soul. Even as today's computers cannot understand the source of their energy, neither can we. To summarize, most of us are "lifers" waiting for retirement and pensions. The problem is they forgot to tell us that a new war has started, and we are the enemy. I wasn't an innocent. I lacked sufficient educational credentials and skills, which left me carrying a huge inferiority complex. Trying to please everyone, I pleased no one—

especially myself. I was forced to accept the knowledge that nothing would change until I took charge of my own needs. I was depressed and physically sick. I knew I needed a change.

Back to School

My intent was to create a back-to-school comedy, but a funny thing happened along the way. I did not find it funny at all. I pursued knowledge seriously. I did not feel like Rodney Dangerfield among kids. I felt like a student studying and learning along with my peers. The big advantage I had was a wealth of experience and life material to draw on—which served me well. I did not have the disruption of dating or overactive hormones to interrupt me. I could cross decades with ease in my essays. The instructors closer to my age would see a reflection of their years in my writings. Writing became a sharing, usually with an "A" for effort. I didn't just read books, I devoured them. *I was a happy man in a play world.* Did I miss society? Not really. I had a world of friends: Willy Loman, King Lear, Gulliver, Conrad, Toni Morrison, and hundreds more. I was in a world filled with interesting people and ideas. What I did miss was the sharing of these worlds with real people who would laugh, cry, and argue with me. I wanted to share but was separated from the instructors by class, and the students by age. I was lonely in a crowded campus. I wanted a literary affair. I wanted something I feared more than failure. I was afraid of this arousal; it begged for more and more. I must keep feeding it as long as my mind allows it. I'm glad I went back to school and am proud of my work and degree.

Education is more than a search for knowledge. It is also a search for self, which cannot be taught. It must be chosen. The real tragedy of my story is that my wife is looking for the same thing, although by a different path. We are on roads divided by a barrier, separating our feelings and desires. The flaws were always inside me, and my parents, and their parents. They were my teachers and leaders. They were a part of my ambition, and my acceptance. I gave my life away years ago. I sold myself piece by piece. It was the cost of the game, and I was a game player. I now have the opportunity to look at what I've become—and what I can be. The key is to broaden and change limits. I must rebuild and not just repaint. My graduation must be into a world of choices. I hope both of us have learned enough of our pasts and potential futures. Because we will cross paths again. Following Dale Carnegie gave me a false sense of security. I had ignored my karma and my soul. Now I am glad both Holly and I understand that following our karma is the only way for us to be together and be whole. One last item, following my graduation from the University of Minnesota, I decided not to return to the corporate world. Instead, I took a job at a Barnes & Noble bookstore. The next twenty years, I was happy and stress-free. My fellow employees and many customers turned into friends, sharing common interests and ideas. I had finally found my niche and was *a happy man in the real world*.

I've always been an American Civil War reader. I have over a hundred volumes in my library, including Shelby Foote and Bruce Catton trilogies. The era was a critical time for our democracy. It is equally relevant today. I have also loved reading and writing poetry. It gives me the freedom to express myself and allows me to imagine anything anytime. With poetry, I can picture another vision of possibilities. *Leaves of Grass Revisited* reflects a vision of history and the possibility of hope and renewal.

This book follows my journey inside. It is not complete; after all, I'm just beginning…

Walt Whitman's

Leaves of Grass Revisited

For Walt
(My mentor and guide)

Prologue

If Walt were around
What would he say?
Would he just smile,
Or be amazed

A time for all ages
Both the good and the bad converging together,
The sane and the mad

Approaching Aquarius
We seem ill prepared
To listen to Walt,
And to take up his dare

Our Civil War spiritual
In our souls, we conflict
Faith is challenged
And visions are mixed

All the good and evil
That ever was—still is
All the hurt and pain
Locked within remain

From the cloud containing
Both the good and bad weather
Into each of our lives
The worst and best come together

I am the God, who
Chooses and selects
I am the God, who
Will serve and protect

I am your karma
As you are mine
Forward or backward
Deciding if, now is the time

Many have walked the path
And many share the bond
Some know the way but
Only a few can pass it on

The answer is in the future
As it was in the past
The message is simple
It's only belief we lack

Thank you, Walt, for telling me
It's okay to take a chance
Thank you, Walt, for showing
The beauty in the dance

To work and to play
For gain and for leisure
To hoard and release
All our pleasures and treasures

To study and to learn
Not to lecture or advice
To feel the knowledge
We are not a compromise

Walt, we're starting over
And need to listen to the past
To understand the reasons for,
What will pass and what will last

I wish you were here to help us
We need a man of age
To bring us a perspective, of
What is fad and what is sage

The children are our challenge
Even more than you and I
They don't buy ambiguity
And rightfully ask why

Folks today are literal
Looking for cause and effect
People now invest and plan
And always hedge their bet

Prophecies don't scare them
They see too much gloom and doom
It's like we are in an oasis
Or an air-conditioned tomb

We don't remember past lives
How our dreams were all the same
The only difference, in reality
Are the places and the names

Our travels are just beginning
A need to go somewhere
Do you want to come along?
A place to care and share

We will change all that we touch
In small and subtle ways
The only thing important
Is that we begin today

Walt will be with us, or
Whomever else you want
Come along, walk with us
Toward the Aquarian front

Adventure

1858–1863

1863

It's been two years since I've been home—too long a time to be away. I joined up at Fort Snelling, wanting to get into the fight before it was all over. I've regretted it ever since, more than a few times. It is now 1863, and we are not far from a small town called Gettysburg. My mind, though, is back home five years earlier.

Richard and George at Home

1858

We were proud as peacocks that day, with Minnesota becoming the thirty-second state to join the Union. My friend George and I were fourteen years old and in awe of the goings-on. Lieutenant Covill was there, leading the reserve group. I remember him saying, "Boys, I am going to be looking for you in a few years. If you can shoot straight, your country will be needing you." Didn't rightly understand what he meant. But we were pickled with pride when he spoke to us—and right in front of Mary Ellen.

Now Mary Ellen was a beauty, only thirteen then, but almost ripe for picking. Her pa, though, watched over her like a hawk. The only time we could talk was walking to and from school. I think she liked me more than George because she always smiled and winked at me when George was pontificating.

How to describe her? I still have the picture she gave me before George and I left for St. Paul. Her eyes were dark yet often lit up in mischief. She was almost as tall as me, which was great for dancing but not so good when we fought. No city girl was she, tanned and strong-willed and willing to work. Her face and body are pretty, although I might be a little prejudiced. Her voice changed as often as her moods, impossible to capture in words. I would get strange feelings when we touched. I guess you can tell by now I'm kind of stuck on her, as is George. We'd prance and dance like flies over an apple pie.

1861

I remember specifically the day we told her we were going to enlist.

"Boys, I never heard such a foolish notion."

"But Mary Ellen, we are going to be the first to hitch up to Lincoln's wagon—ain't you proud?" said George.

"Proud of what? Getting yourselves shot someplace we've never heard of."

"Heavens, you two aren't even old enough."

"Yes, we will be—at least on the scrap of paper with the number eighteen that we put in the bottom of our shoes."

Besides, Lieutenant Hawkins said we will get a hundred-dollar bonus, and George and I feel it's our duty to defend the Union and free the poor Negroes from slaveholders. I had added that for Mary Ellen's benefit, as I knew she and her family were staunch abolitionists. "But Richard, who will take care of the farm? Your Pa's been sickly, and Billy's too young."

"Mary Ellen, don't be a ninny. Pa can manage and get Luke's help as needed. Besides, he told us to chase the Secesh back to hell where they belong."

"Mary Ellen, Richard, and I got orders to report on Friday. The recruiter's wagon will be picking us up. You got to come see us off—I must go, I promised Ma."

After George left, Mary Ellen was silent for the longest time. I kept quiet 'cause she didn't need me to help her think. Although only sixteen, she was the maturest person I knew. I'd never tell her, but I respected her smarts more than anything. In that way, she was like my mama, always reading and writing stuff. She said, "Let's sit by the pond for a while."

I thought, *Oh! I'm in big trouble because Mary Ellen sits about as often as a hummingbird in spring.*

"Richard, I know you and George are going, and maybe it's right. But I can't feel good about it." "I've never told anyone about this, but I have dreams."

In one, I saw George lying on the ground by a river or creek. Everything looked dark and quiet. I could hear him crying. You know how he is, all teeth and bones. I am counting on you to watch over him and keep him on the right track. In another dream, you and I were sitting in a big boat. You were dressed in black and me in white. Around us were children playing and laughing. It was odd the way they were dressed. We approached a big city with tall buildings made of glass. I remember the sunlight reflecting off them. I turned to you, and you faded away, saying "Tomorrow, tomorrow." Then you were gone.

Mary Ellen cried, and I felt her move into my arms. I kissed her, and we touched softly. I can't describe the feeling. I didn't know what to do. "Mary Ellen, you know I love you and honor you and will do anything you ask."

"Richard, be quiet, please." We must have laid that way for hours if my numb arm was any proof. "This is my goodbye. I will not be there on Friday, but I expect you to write. I don't have much to give you except this old key chain, which was my grandpa's. Promise me you will carry it always."

"Yes, Mary Ellen, I will."

"Tell George goodbye for me."

"Mary Ellen, I'm sorry I got carried away. I don't know what got into me. I love you, and we're going to get married as soon as I get back."

"Richard, don't worry, we will let time and nature prove our love. No need to rush. I'll be here today and tomorrow—just write and write a lot." As she went away, I was in a tumble.

Leaving for St. Paul

1861

"Where have you been, boys? I hope the army teaches you some responsibility. I have never seen two boys who spend so much time talking, and so little doing. Dreams don't milk the cows or mow the hay. Lincoln knew that. This land is made of sweat and common sense. Go help your Mama. No need to waste your last night at home."

"Can I go see them off?" Billy said.

"I don't care if you get back by nine. You might find it interesting—what kind of crop the army's picking. Hope they are riper than Richard. Ma, Pa said you need some help."

"Yes, I do, Richard. Come sit with me and help with the potatoes."

"Ah, Ma, that's boy's work."

"You might as well get used to it. I heard armies only travel on a full stomach. Richard, I just want to talk."

"Yes, Ma, I know."

"I sewed up your jacket. I don't think you will need the winter one as the army will outfit you. I also packed your knapsack with extra socks and drawers and some vittles for the road. Also, I hid a gold piece in your belt for an emergency. Most importantly, I packed the Lord's Word, and I want you to read it often. I raised you as a Christian boy. Heaven knows what kind of riffraff you'll run into, but I know God's words will lead and comfort you, as they comfort me."

"Yes, Mama."

Pa walked in. "That's right, Mother, you arm him with prayer, and I'll provide the gun. I know you can shoot right good."

"But, Pa, that's your new gun for hunting."

"Don't worry, boy, I suspect it will get more use hunting Secesh than rabbits. Take it and show them Rebs what a Minnesota boy can do."

The next morning, George was over by 7:00 a.m., raring to go. What can I say about George? We all have special friends, and he was mine. The kind of guy you can hunt and fish with, or just enjoy doing nothing when you are together. George's Pa and Ma came over from Germany in '49 and settled here by error. They were supposed to go farther west, but Mrs. Mueller put her foot down and said, "No farther—we will stay here where God put us." They don't speak much American, but George's father will go to the grave before admitting it was her idea.

Anyway, George said, "Your father gave you his gun? Shit, my Pa never even said 'Auf Wiedersehen.'"

"Watch your swearing, George. We don't want to begin our trip with a licking. Let's get going; the wagons are going to be here soon. They won't wait for stragglers."

As we got to the square, I saw Lieutenant Hawkins on his brown mare. "I see you aren't chickens after all. You look more like hayseeds than Union soldiers, but never mind, I'm going to whip you into shape—that's my job. This here is Sergeant Svensson, regular army since '54. He will take care of you like your mama. Right, sergeant?"

"Yes, sir, but I don't know how Col. Gorman expects me to make a regiment out of these bare-assed, dun-dripping, fly-crawling garbage like this."

"That's your job, Sergeant. I expect them to look and act like soldiers before we reach St. Paul for the mustering. Do what you must, short of shooting them all."

"Yes, sir." The lieutenant rode off. I thought, just like Hawkins to put on airs like somebody important. He looked like a general with all the silk, feathers, gold buttons, and sword. Despite my disgust, I would give my right arm for his horse. I must admit he looked like an officer. I knew from experience; however, that he was dumber than the horse he sat on. "George, my advice to you is to watch and listen to the lieutenant—and then do the opposite. My gut is telling me he couldn't lead an Indian to a whiskey bottle, let alone us in battle."

"What are you girls gawking at? Ain't you ever seen a horse's ass before? All you have got to do is look into a mirror. Now line up and stand at attention." George and I were joined by Remer Johnson. I thought Remer would be the last to enlist. He was a preacher's son and fatter than a milking cow. "Boys, here's what we're gonna do: each of you sign this paper. It says we ain't stealing you from your Mama's tit. It allows us to transport you in this here wagon. We will make several stops along the way to pick up a few more virgins before Fort Snelling. Any questions? Good, now get your lily-white asses into the wagon. I'll ride in the front with Corporal Olesen so I don't have to smell you all the way."

George said, "Ain't he a sweetheart, just like Pa, only in American. Hey, Remer, what are you doing here?"

"I d-don't know. My d-daddy w-wanted me to represent G-God among the b-boys. It's also m-mission to spread the w-word of G-God to the slaves we f-free."

So be it, I thought. What an army, an idiot lieutenant leading a foulmouthed sergeant into battle with two hayseeds and an evangelist who stutters. The Secesh better look out, or we will cuss, pray, and stink them to death. I'm not going to describe the whole trip. Suffice it to say, we picked up many more converts and ended up packed tighter than flies on a cow's back.

At Fort Snelling, Minnesota

1861

"George, we've reached the promised land."
"What?"
"Never mind—look…"

The fort was alive with soldiers and recruits. Men marching, sitting, and lying about everywhere. "Get down, girls, and stretch your pretty legs. The army's anxious to pick your cherries before you change your minds—little though they be. Line up and follow me. Don't even try to march. They will laugh me out of camp. Just shut up and do what I do—except for the scratching. You ain't been here long enough to get the itch. Captain, sir, twenty-three new recruits reporting and right eager to join Lincoln's Army."

"Thank you, Sergeant. Where is Lieutenant Hawkins?"

"I believe he stopped to pick up some necessities and will be along shortly."

"All right, Sergeant. Let the boys have some vittles, and we will muster in at 1800 hours in the big hall. You're excused. Good luck, men."

"All right, boys, it's time to feed the dogs. Keep your gear with you as not everyone is as honest as your sarg and your mama."

There had to be more than one hundred in the mess room.

We sat at long tables set in rows. "Dick, do you see that?"

"What, George?"

"That Negro over by the officers' table."

I looked quickly; I had never seen a real live Negro before. He looked like an Indian with short curly hair. "George, he looks a lot like Remer."

"Yup, you're right. Hey, Remer, I found your first convert." Remer looked like he wanted to crawl under the table.

"Quiet, guys, he might hear us. I can't preach until I learn their language." George saw Sergeant Svendsen walking by. "Hey, Sarg, when do we eat?"

"What's your name, maggot?"

"I'm George, one of the Mankato boys, remember?"

"Oh yes, of course. If you boys will follow me, I'll see what we can do to speed the cook ahead."

Walking with him, I felt a premonition of trouble ahead.

"Hey, O'Hara, I have two future generals with me who say they are hungry. Can you help them?"

"Surely as night begets day. I'll do everything I can for the poor starving lads. If you haven't guessed, I'm Irish and proud of it. I brought all the potatoes all the way from my mother's garden in Dublin. She blessed each one in the name of the Holy Virgin Mother, Mary. What I need you to do is to circumcise them, carefully peeling away the foreskins, just as Father O'Hara is showing you. This is a sacred religious rite, and you boys should be honored."

"I knew it, George. From now on, let me do the talking. I hope you are happy with our first military engagement. Darn, I cut my finger."

"I'm sorry, I didn't know."

"Shut up and pass the spuds."

The food that night wasn't half bad, although we didn't get served like the officers. I recognized Capt. Covill. After dinner was messed up, another captain stood up… Attention!

"My name is Captain Nelson, Regular Army, USA. You are about to join the First Minnesota Regiment as promised by Governor Ramsey personally to Abraham Lincoln on April thirteenth.

You are over one thousand men strong, and I proudly announce you will be part of the first three-year volunteers. You and I know we never picked this fight. The Rebs have been taunting us, taking federal forts, and tearing down the flags of our forefathers. In the name of King Cotton, they want to rip asunder our glorious Union. As slavery is an abomination, so are they. As free men, we will fight to keep the Union whole and free. Today is May 23, 1861, and by volunteering, you have earned the right to fight treason and rebellion. I doubt if it will take very long to convince them of the error in their ways. Equally important, you will have honored your state, country, and God. Now if you will all raise your right hand and swear after me. So help you, God."

"I welcome you to the United States Army. Although only soldiers in name yet, your officers and non-coms will be training you in one of the regiments of the Army of the Potomac. The flag you walk under has been stained with generations of glory. I expect each of you to guard and protect the colors of your life. God bless you all."

"Wow," George said. "I ain't never heard so many big words coming together like that."

Seeing Sergeant Svendsen, I ducked until I heard, "I want this table to follow me. You are now part of Company F, in command of your good friend Lieutenant Hawkins. Your barracks is a big building with the 'F' on it. Do you get it?"

An hour later, we were well settled and going through some meager army issues. "What are we going to do with all this stuff? I can't carry it all, along with all the things from home."

"I know, George, I'm in the same boat. Hey, Lieutenant, what can we do with all this? It's too much."

"Toss some away."

"What do we toss?"

"I don't know. I'll check and get back to you."

I knew as sure as God made rain, we wouldn't hear back from Hawkins.

The next few weeks went by quickly. We drilled, drilled, and drilled some more.

The sergeant was on us like a blanket over a rug. I learned to respect his experience and to watch him anticipate trouble. He held a low opinion of officers, except General McClellan, whom he had previously served under. We also met a passel of characters from all over Minnesota, the Dakotas, and Iowa.

One odd one was Travis Macomber. Previously, he had been a scout and fought both the Sioux and the Cheyenne. He told us about Indian fighting and how once he had killed three braves with only a knife. He said he was once married to a squaw and showed us a purse that he said was made from a woman's teat. I don't know; it didn't look like much to me. When he offered to trade it for my jacket, I began to doubt his stories. Regardless, he was impressive looking. I thought if things got too hot, he would be a good man to stand behind.

Remer, it appears, had finally met the Negro and was shocked to find the man was called Thaddius and had been raised as a freedman, educated by the Quakers in Pennsylvania. He spoke God's Words just like the Bible, full of *thees* and *thous*. I often see them together, reading and talking. They look a lot like brothers. George is doing well. He takes to soldiering like a duck to water. The only sore spot is his gambling. He is already in debt up to next month's pay. I told him not to come knocking on my door when he's broke. I see whiskey and gambling as the devil's agent and active in this man's army. Two days ago, a man from another company got so drunk he shot and killed a Negro in camp. I heard he got fifteen days (about two weeks) in the guardhouse and was fined thirteen dollars. "Damn it, Richard, you've gotten uppity since you got that letter from Mary Ellen. I don't think it's right you're not sharing her words with me. I know she wrote to me also, but I think you and her got secrets."

Dear Mary Ellen,
June 25, 1861

    I received your letter last week, and George is jealous. It's hard to believe it's only been a short time since we parted. So much has happened. They had a banquet for the whole regiment at Nicollet Island. I have never seen so much food. Please take a photo and send it to me. You know I will treasure it as I treasure you. I was afraid you'd forget me as soon as I left. I heard we will be going east soon. They said we would take a boat to La Crosse and then a train to Chicago and eastward. I'm excited and looking forward to testing our mettle against the Rebs. Know that I think of you always. Write soon. Send lots of letters. Please, please, please.

Yours truly,
Richard

Going East

1861

Dear Ma and Pa,

    I promised you I'd drop a note. George and I are fine and busy. We are real soldiers now and ready for battle. Sergeant Svendsen is like a father to us, and Captain Covill is smart and experienced. We are getting ready to go East. I'll write to you again from there.
    Say hi to Billy.

Respectfully,
Your son, Richard

It's now June 27, and we are in Chicago waiting for a train to take us further. Sarg and I are sharing a pipe (yes, I smoke). "Richard, I've been in many fixes in my life, and I've learned to look for people who can help me when the going gets tough. I think of people like horses—you got your chargers, thoroughbreds, and gaiters. Now Travis and George are chargers who will run fast but fade if the race is long. Hawkins and Remer are thoroughbreds, pretty but not very good when it comes to digging in the mud. You and I are gaiters. We will wait and evaluate and pace ourselves for the long haul. I just want you to know I'll have your back if you have mine."

    "Well, Sarg, I'm mighty honored that you would spend so many words on me, and not a cussword among them. My thought, though, is to pretty much take care of myself and George. Let everyone else fight their own battles. You may be right about horses, but I don't know what I will do. I suspect I'll do what everyone else does—fight when they fight and run when they run."

"Hells Bells. Nobody knows, including the colonel. None of you boys have faced a real army. I'll tell you, the Rebs will fight and fight well. I've met a few, and a meaner bunch of cusses you will never know. Rank is in your balls, not on your sleeve. Remember what I told you…"

As Sarg left, I thought, *What's got into him?* I've never seen a man turn from a muleskinner to a philosopher so quickly. Maybe it's due to the summer heat.

"What's your name, private?"

"Hawkins, you know me."

"Me what?"

"Oh Christ, me, sir."

"That's better. I can see it is going to be a lot of work to turn you into a real soldier. Get down off that horse, and I'll show you…"

"Insubordination, Sarg. Put this boy on the report. I'll have you walking picket duty from here to Richmond. Now get on the train and out of my hair." On the train, we went. Endless boredom, constant chatter, and rumor after rumor—about drove me nuts. To get my mind off everything, I pulled out Mary Ellen's letter and photo.

Dear Richard,

> I thank the Lord you and George are doing fine. Send him my love and prayers. I've thought about what we said and didn't say by the pond. I don't feel bad at all. My dreams have stopped and are replaced by a quiet confidence in my man (you).
>
> I know I was being foolish and smitten with fear—that has been transformed into real love. I'm calm now in the way of all women. Your love has enabled me to cast off my childhood and prepare for the adult world. I'm knitting you a sweater today, a loving task. I hope you will wear

it always close to your heart, as I hold your photo next to mine.

Your love,
Mary Ellen

I'm puzzled by her letter. I've never seen her in this mood before. It's almost like the further I am away, the stronger her love gets. Maybe I should go to France or something. I hope Mary Ellen never finds out I showed it to George. I couldn't resist seeing his face. I think he was less affected than he pretended. He has found a new love—Lady Luck, and she has seduced him quicker than a two-bit whore on payday.

The Army of the Potomac

1861–1865

We arrived in Alexandria, Virginia, on July 3 and disembarked en masse to take our quarters. I've never seen so many officers. George and I quit saluting about halfway through the day. I don't think they care. On Sunday, we all got a furlough, and I went to see the White House and Lincoln. He wasn't there, but we saw Seward over by the State Department. We also met some fellows from the Third Massachusetts, Ed Kennedy and Frank Barnes were their names. Both were part of the Third's Band and Chorus group. "Come with us tonight. You boys will hear music sweeter than meat off a lobster."

"What's a lobster?" George asked.

"Come with us to Williams for a real treat."

Although apprehensive, I was curious to see if it measured up to the freshwater fish back home. "My name is Richard, and this no-count with me is George. He is a chef in Minnesota and won a Blue Ribbon at the state fair for carp à la cream."

"What's carp?"

"Well, that is a story for another day. Lead on, Macduff."

I must admit, these Boston boys sure knew a good thing. George had two lobsters, and we quaffed a few pints to allow the culture of Boston to settle properly. "Edward and Frank, I sure hope we meet again."

"Goes double for us. It's nice to know someone appreciates culture west of the Mississippi. Say, how did your regiment get sent way out here?"

"We don't rightly know, but I suspect Lincoln wanted all the soldiers he could get twixt him and Richmond, and we were volunteered."

"I heard the army's massing for a big battle soon."

"Yes, and if you boys are looking for the front of the battle, look for the Third Mass colors"

When we got back to camp, I could see we were stripping for a move. They issued rations for three days and one hundred rounds of minié balls. Fifty or so of company K are not coming as they don't have army pants yet. "They said, 'We ain't fighting the Rebs bare-assed.'" I guess I don't blame them. Although we missed most of the concert, I could hear music as we left camp. "John Brown's body lies a-moldering in his grave. His soul is marching on."

Seeing The Elephant

1861

Dear Pa and Ma,

Well, we have seen our first battle with the Rebs at Bull Run (they call it Manassas). I have to say we got licked. Our regiment alone lost 150 killed and wounded, including Lieutenant Hawkins. He drew bullets like a bee to honey, what with his fancy coat and yellow scarf. Although he died bravely, I grieve as much for the mare as for the man. Lieutenant William Lochren is now company commander. He seems a decent sort. George and I are both fine; don't worry, next time we will lick them. Say hi to Billy.

Your Son,
Richard.

"Hey, Dick, I'm hungry. Why don't you stroll to the sutler's tent and get some of that new-fangled canned stuff, and maybe some ginger cakes?"
"You got any money?"
"No."
"I'm going to stop by the hospital and see how Remer is doing. He had been taken down sick just before Bull Run."
"Hey, Remer, how are you doing?"
"Hi, Thaddius."
"Not so loud, Richard, if not for Thaddius's soup I'd starve."

"Remer, you didn't miss much the other day. We spent most of the time chasing our own army back to the battle. I have never seen so much confusion. McDowell's got to go. Right, Thaddius?"

"Surely, Master Richard, if it wasn't for the Minnesota boys, thee'd be in a rebel hospital today."

"Richard, Thaddius has been reading to me from *Uncle Tom's Cabin*. He is going to be in a theatrical show next month. He says he can get me a part too."

"Great, Remer, I'll look forward to a great thespian career for you two. Hope you get better soon."

Thaddius and I left the tent. "How's he really doing?"

"I don't know. He can't seem to lick the fever and keeps getting weaker and weaker. I'm afraid he might not pull through. You know how much I love him. He has treated me like a human being from the beginning."

"I know, Thaddius. You've given Remer something he has never had before—a real friend. Take good care of him and let me know how things go. I'll write to his folks. God be with you, Thaddius."

"Yes, and with thee."

Dear Mary Ellen,

> How are you doing? Sorry it's been so long since I've written, but it has been hectic here. Remer died. He never saw a battle and never freed a slave. His best friend was a Negro who loved and cared for him. Maybe that's his redemption. In late July, we had a Review of the Grand Army at Harrison's Landing. Lincoln was there, but I only saw his top hat. Otherwise, things have been quiet, marching, drilling, and picket duty. I'm subsisting on a diet of hardtack, coffee, and pork and beans. I'll write again soon. Got to go now as they are beating the drums to move out.
>
> Sincerely,
> Richard

The fall and winter of '61 passed without too much happening. All in all, not a bad life. It's easy not to have to choose. The men have bonded well together for good and bad. The Minnesota boys seem to be the most talented and energetic in the army. In October, we helped the army to bridge the Potomac by driving boats. Call me Commodore Richard now.

Discovery and Disillusionment

1862

I'm not going to relate a thousand conversations with hundreds of men. Each was a thread in forming a blanket of friendships. My closest friends were Sergeant Svendsen, Lieutenant Lochren, Thaddius, Travis, Edward, and (when I could see them) the Taylor boys from Company C. George also, but he is more of a brother than a friend. People come to me a lot with their homesickness and other complaints. They seem to think I understand, and maybe sometimes I do. They trust my judgment and common sense. If they really knew, they'd see me more as a dreamer. I constantly imagine I'm not here. I feel like a visitor to this time and place.

Dear Ma and Pa,

It is summer, and nothing good has happened. Old Stonewall is chasing us all over the place. Most of McClellan's army, including us, is retreating toward the James River. After the slaughter at Savage Station, where we lost another forty-eight men just in a rear action. This war is getting deadly, without any visible gain. We need a Lee or a Jackson on our side. Regardless, I have faith that we will stay the course.

Your son,
Richard

*****

Dear Mary Ellen,

    George is dead. I wish I were too. It happened in a rear-guard action, and he got caught in the crossfire. George is dead. There is nothing more I can say. I'm going to miss him so much. I never told him how much I loved him—now it's too late. I didn't even get to hold him. He was cold before we noticed him missing. I just want to sleep and get my mind back together.

Love,
Richard

*****

Dear Richard,

    I received your letter about George and have cried for him and for us. I would have written sooner, but it's been crazy here. The Sioux have risen up and massacred almost the entire town of New Ulm. I've been told over three hundred men, women, and children were killed. The rumor is the Indian agent stole or held back their food, saying, "Let them eat grass." He was found later dead with grass stuffed in his mouth. Don't worry about our safety, as the Sioux have fled. Colonel Sibley and the Third Minnesota have been called to chase the renegades. George's ma and pa were among the killed. Maybe it's a blessing they will never know about George. Richard, I'm more frightened for you. Your letter sounded different, cold, and hard. Are you that way now? I wish we could turn back the clock to bring us together again, but I can't. All I can do is ask you to take care of yourself first! I've been praying every night. Your mama and I are good friends now, and we talk often about you. She tells me stories, and we read together, as she said you and her used to do. I feel she has adopted me. Please know I am not taking your place but only holding a place for you, next to me.

Love,
Mary Ellen

Disillusionment

1862

It's been a year of death; I'd just as soon not remember. Two words stick on my tongue: *Antietam* and *Fredericksburg*. One a slaughter, the other a massacre. Our regiment lost 147 men at Antietam. And our Second Corps lost almost four thousand at Fredericksburg.

What a horror! I heard from Pa that Sibley caught over one thousand Indians and that thirty-eight were hanged. Maybe that's right and proper, but I feel we should hang thirty-eight of our generals for what they have done to us. Sergeant and I were talking the other day, and he said, "Sometimes I think the only reason we've survived so far is that we are always at the front of the front—too close for the Rebs to charge or their artillery to hit us without hitting their own men. It also seems to me that battles have little to do with generals and planning. They ask us to fight when we should run and run when we should stand. It's like Lee has us on a string, and we keep following and biting his heels until he decides when and where to turn and slap us upside the head." My thoughts are jumbled, but I'm coming to an understanding that God is not on either side. I've seen the good die and the bad live. I've seen luck save some and kill others. I've witnessed stupidity succeed where reason fails. It's like God is indifferent. I want to go home. I'm crying now. I don't care anymore.

Tenting on the Old Campground

We're tenting tonight, tenting on the old campground
Give us a song to cheer
For our weary hearts, a song of home

And the friends we love so dear
Many are the hearts that are weary tonight
Waiting for the war to cease
Many are the hearts looking for the right
To see the dawn of peace…

Renewal

1863

> Some place in Maryland
> Rally round the flags, boys
> Rally once again
> Shouting the battle cry of freedom
> The Union forever, hurrah, boys, hurrah
> Down with sedition, up with the star.

The new boys are singing this song. They haven't seen the *elephant* yet. They are anxious and scared. "Right, lieutenant?" Right, if the music were Minie balls, the war would be long over. They'd better be ready. I saw Col. Covill and heard them talking about the Rebs coming North again. Lee must be hungry and looking for Northern vittles. At least we got fighting men now like General Hancock. "Hello, Minnesota. How are you doing?" It was Edward Kennedy, whom I hadn't seen since that God-awful Chancellorsville.

"Frank caught it there. I heard George died also."

"That's right, Ed. Let's go talk."

Edward's story was pretty much like my own and everyone else's. I heard we are moving out to shadow Lee's army. I also heard Hooker's been replaced by Meade. "I thought they were done replacing generals. Who is Meade? Is he any good? I don't know, but he is from Pennsylvania, and that seems where Lee is headed. We both know the real general is Lincoln. It's too bad he can't soldier as well as he politics. Edward, I must say this falls on me like a wet blanket, but there ain't much I can do about it. Let's talk about something else."

"When this war is over, I want you to come to visit me and my family. My sister Lynne is seventeen years old now and would love to meet wild Westerners. Promise me you will come."

"Yes, on one condition."

"What's that?"

"You will have to reciprocate and visit Mankato. You will love fishing, wild game, and beautiful vistas. All we must do is get through '63, and our terms are up. I'm not re-signing, are you?"

"Hell no, I've seen and done enough. I just want to go home. I'll say a few 'Ave Marias' for both of us. Maybe the Virgin Mary will make an exception for you. I will ask Luther to do the same for one drunken Irishman." We will meet again in Richmond.

Gettysburg Eve

July 1, 1863

Dear Ma, Pa, and Mary Ellen,

    We have been marching all over Maryland and now Pennsylvania, following Lee's army. We don't know where they are, but fortunately, they don't know where we are either. Last night, Col. Covill was arrested. It appears someone got upset because we were smart enough to use some timbers to cross a creek instead of soaking our shoes and pants. The army didn't take kindly to our thinking. Ain't too serious though. I expect he will rejoin us tomorrow. We are moving toward Gettysburg, where it looks like everyone is headed. I'm glad everyone is fine at home. Don't worry. It looks like we will be in reserve, well behind the fighting. Ma, thank you for taking Mary Ellen under your wing. I expect to be home by spring and will help Pa and Billy with the planting. Mary Ellen, I needn't say how anxious I am for our future together.

With love,
Richard

Meeting My Guide

July 1, 1863

I am telling you my letter was a sham. Yes, we were supposed to be in reserve, but this battle is going to need everyone. I also didn't tell them how I had twisted my shoulder out of the joint and how it hurts like crazy. I'm sitting by a tree near the medical tent. They told me to grin and bear it. I know they have bigger problems on their hands. The wagons have been rolling all day. More frightening is a feeling that's been creeping up on me, something I can't shake off.

"Hello, young man. I'm Walt Whitman, lately of Manhattan. What's your name?"

I am Richard from Minnesota. "I've heard of you boys. A finer bunch of Western manhood was never assembled. Mind if I sit a spell with you? Are you hurting bad?"

"No, it's just my arm. Ain't nothing to keep me here except to rest a bit."

"Well, that sounds good. I need a rest myself. I'm too old for all this tramping about. I've met many a soldier, and I can tell you're hurting more than just your arm. Am I right?"

"You are right. They told me you can't fool a guide."

"What are you saying?"

"First, let me tell you I don't think I'm crazy. I've kind of been expecting you. I have a message they told me to give to you. I don't think our meeting up is a chance. You see, Mr. Whitman, I am dying tomorrow. I'm saying it as a fact, not a fear. I'm not sad but disappointed about all the things I'll miss. I know this sounds silly, but I would appreciate your humoring me on this."

"Richard, I'll do much more than humor you. I don't understand all of it, but I've felt this kind of connection in my writing. As a poet, I believe with every fiber of my being that we are connected."

"Mr. Whitman, I know you are not a preacher, but would you be embarrassed in praying for my soul?"

"Not at all, boy. Hold my hand, and let's pray together. Richard, I will gladly take the message and honor it and you."

"Would you do something for me?"

"Yes, what is it?"

"Please take this golden key of mine with you tomorrow. I've had it for years but don't feel it's mine anymore. I hope it will do for you what it's done for me. I love you, boy, and we will meet again—I promise."

Dear Mary Ellen,

I'm not much for words, but I must write this down before the Guide comes. I know he and I are connected. Last night, I received a vision. They told me to write it down and give it to the white-haired man, who is also a Guide. Mary Ellen, they won't let me sleep. Maybe I am already dead. Tell Mama that whenever I got homesick or scared, I would remember her songs and stories. Tell Billy not to sign up. Lincoln's got enough blue bodies. I am crying like a baby now, but I don't care. A man's got a right to cry before he dies. I'll miss you, Mary Ellen, so much. Pray for my soul. I know we will be together again. I've got to stop now, but I have all the numbers down. They told me it was very important. Our future is still ahead, Mary Ellen. So I will not say goodbye until we meet again. I am writing this to you. I think you are the only one who will understand what is happening to me. There was a big battle today and an even bigger one coming tomorrow.

Things are very strange for me. I received a vision from a Guide, foretelling a future for you and me. I know you have also received visions and will understand. The Guide has given me a message to pass along. Mary Ellen, I just want to say I love you, and the Guide has promised we will be together again. Do not be afraid or sad. I know things will happen which will make things right for you and me, and our future family.

Love as always,
Richard

Gettysburg—the End?

July 2, 1863

It's *tomorrow* already, and we have been sitting here since early morning, looking out toward the area where Sickles's Third Corps has moved out. The battle was fierce all day. I don't have any idea who is winning. I'm happy to be here, and not there. It's going to be nightfall soon, and maybe things will settle down. "God damn, boys, close up! It looks like Humphreys' men have broken!" There was pandemonium all around us. I could see waves of Blue running on our left, straight back to Cemetery Hill. I also see a whole passel of Rebs moving up toward Plum Run. That's General Hancock over there, talking to Col. Covill—I can feel it coming… "Come on, First Minnesota, we're going to charge those Rebels and push them back! Let's go now!" I charged out behind Svendsen and silently said good-bye to his back.

God, I feel good
My blood's a-pumping and
My arm doesn't hurt anymore
Looking at the lieutenant and Travis
They don't look scared either
I just want to run faster
No, slow down
Nothing's gonna stop us
Lieutenant, don't stop
Can't do him any good
Ain't no sense in shooting
Don't want too anyway
Think I'll just run into

That bunch over there
God, it's funny
They look scared
Of me?
Here I come, boys
I'm shot
Don't hurt too bad, damn, again
Can't stand up
Help me, Reb
Help me get up
Jesus—he is
Gonna kill me.

Epilogue

The Battle of Gettysburg lasted three days, with almost fifty thousand men killed or wounded, North and South. The Civil War went on another two years, at the cost of almost six hundred thousand lives—Americans all. The First Minnesota was an honored regiment in the Army of the Potomac. The charge at Gettysburg occurred on July 2 and cost them over 112 men killed or wounded out of the 268 men who made the charge. The next day, another seventeen men were lost repulsing Pickett's Charge. Does any of this matter? I don't know if anyone, even Lincoln, can consecrate truly honor these men.

> Maybe a poet can honor them, not with
> a eulogy but with a promise.
> I bequeath myself to the dirt
> To grow from the grass I love
> If you want to see me again, look for me
> Under your boot soles
> You will hardly know who I am
> Or what I mean
> But I shall be good health
> To you, nevertheless, and
> Filter and fiber, your blood
> Failing to fetch me at first
> Keep encouraged
> Missing me one place
> Search another
> I stop somewhere
> Waiting for you.
>
> From *Leaves of Grass* by
> Walt Whitman

A Poem from Richard to Walt

1863

Walt, I was with you
Though I doubt you remember me
I was the one who took your hand
Under the old oak tree
Your eyes were clouded
And mine were red
As we quietly prayed
I can still hear the songs
Blue lines marching, and
Tents covering the ground
I can hear the guns, loud
As if to cover up the sorrow
For the many cold and dead
Who will be buried tomorrow

You passed among the wounded
Most would never get better
We exchanged some small talk
And I gave you a Message
My pain was like a mirror
Reflecting a premonition
I saw in your eyes
My life and condition.

I said to you, take
This Message and pass it on
Don't care if you read it

Since I'll be dead and gone
Knowing I was to die
I wanted to run and hide
But you held my hand
And I saw the golden key
You said, don't worry
This will make you free
I put it in my pocket
And died at Gettysburg
I can still feel the darkness
And the cold damp earth

The Message 1863

One Page of Binary Codes

The Message Decoded

1987

You see, I've finally
Translated the Message
Why now I think you know
The answer was hidden
Deep in a binary code.

It's funny it took me years
To realize the simple fact
The key is not mine to keep
It's time I give it back

So, Walt, I've been looking for you
I've kept you near my heart
I'm very anxious to see you
We've been too long; worlds apart

The answer was an awareness
That the Gold was in the soul
When the circle is unbroken
Between the young and the old

The cycles never-ending
Perfection is not the key
Reality is in imagining
What is and what can be

The future we envision
Is guided by the past
The answers are not in the stars
But more in looking back

The Prophecy

Two is the number
Not only a pair
Two is the multiplier
To show how we care

Two is a symbol we are not alone
Side by side we move
To forgive and atone

Two thousand is destiny
End times on the way
Darkness in the heavens
Night into day

Two worlds will collide
Many will die
And many more cry
There's nowhere to hide

Twin stars will appear
Visible from far and near
Our leaders will face fear
And the people will hear

Messages will arrive and grow
Many stories will be told
Of keys made of solid gold
Allowing futures to unfold

Two will lead
Their visions now a seed
One west, one east
Many will be freed

The time is coming
Good and bad weather
Barometers of the feeling
That will bring us together

Gone will be the limits and judgments of self
Gone will be the hatred
We bring unto ourselves

The new age is Aquarian
In more ways than one
The future's in the tides
And not in the gun

The ebb and flow of souls
Backward and forward in time
Guiding and connecting
All of mankind

By pairs the linking
Guides open the doors
By pairs an imagining, of
A better world and more

The key is to unlock and open
A spiral path reaching high
The key is in connecting
With you and your guide

Short Stories

Richard Dean Holmberg

And there are in our existence
Spots of time.

—William Wordsworth

Terry

They were Catholics, and we knew them well as
friends and neighbors; except on Sundays.
It was the same every week. Terry would lead
the procession, I can see him clearly,
even today. He looked like Mickey Rooney, although
darker. He always wore a white shirt and black pants,
which hung loosely on his short chubby frame. His
shoes were also black, with thick soles, and
a belt too long, with its excess hanging in front like a
tail on backward. A stranger might say he looked
foreign, almost Asiatic; it was not something one wanted to be
labeled as in the time of the Korean War and McCarthyism.
Regardless, Terry was my best friend. I knew, even then, he
was part boy and half man, but it was only in living with his
flaws that I was able to survive my own. I never told him how
much I loved him, even when I knew I was growing away.
It is still Sunday in my mind. I see Terry's brothers following him
out the door. They are big Irishmen in blue/black suits, looking
like overgrown altar boys. They would flank Terry on the way to
the car like an honor guard. The brothers could have been heroes
to me but were too far distant in age and ability for me to idolize.
I heard later that one became a track star and coach, and the other
an air force general working on *Star Wars*. I must confess
the one I was really waiting to see was Terry's
sister, Patty. She was the one I secretly coveted, even on Sundays.
Patty was a Madonna, with long flowing black hair, freckles, and
the small breasts of my dreams. When she would look my way and
smile, I would bow my head in shame, for the wanting I knew
would come, though it was still years away. Turning my mind
back again, I see their mother trailing the procession, seemingly

in a shadowy silence, holding a string of black beads, as if to ward off some evil. It was the same every week. I was fascinated by their Sunday rituals and by the secrets I could not understand.

It all reminds me of another time and place. My friend Dave and I were accosted by two Jehovah's Witnesses on the Old Soldiers' Home bridge. Separating us on opposite sides, they asked us to *kneel* with them in prayer. I refused to *kneel*. I felt betrayed when, looking across the bridge, I saw my friend on his knees. Later, I asked him why, and he said, "I don't know. It just seemed easier than arguing."
It all means nothing to me now, but I remember my disgust and vowed never to *kneel* to anyone.

The images come to me from a distance, as something I grew away from many years ago. Terry, seeing me behind a bush, would run ahead shouting, "Dickie, Dickie." I can feel the love as he would hug and shake me up and down. Even so, I was embarrassed and wanted to hide. You see, Terry was a mongoloid (Down syndrome), and he was my best friend. We were both children together, and both of us had flaws, not understood by either of us. Terry didn't care when I was embarrassed or mean, or when I lied and was ashamed to be near him. Things for Terry were not right or wrong, or unfair—they just were. I didn't know anything about love back then. I'm not sure I know more today.

The times were different. It was the fifties, and I grew up with David and Ricky Nelson and the Beaver. Eisenhower was president, and everyone we knew had a job, plenty of food, and big plans for the future. Of course, I remember the A-bomb and crawling under our school desks. It all seemed like a game for us kids. Real problems were something "out there" and not a part of the Nelson family. Such things were not spoken of in front of children. People were more private back then. Even today, I am still puzzled by the need for confession and self-help. They seem to be a form of public masturbation for private pleasure.

I remember a different time. Bill Haley and the Comets, saddle shoes, poodle skirts, and riding my bike anywhere without a helmet, and often no hands. I remember my older sisters with curlers tucked into their hair with little strips of cloth or Kleenex hanging in a hundred directions. They remind me now of a chorus from some Medusaean tragedy. We had a turtle named Myrtle, who ended up under the wheel of a passing car. We also had a parrot called Pinky, who was killed under the foot of a careless uncle one Christmas Eve. In retrospect, it seems everyone was under somebody's foot. Maybe that's life, even in the Fabulous Fifties.

Dinners at our house were the same every week.
They were a trial and a ritual. They always began
with that god-awful Norwegian prayer.

In Jesu navn
Gatra vita bord
At spise drikke
Pala ord
Gut til haere
Osa til gaun
Sa fotta v matta
N Jesu navn
Amen
Then the vegetables, always the vegetables.
"Eat them or go to bed"
I d-dont like t-them
"Eat or you will sit here all night"
I c-cant
"Don't you dare gag"
"Oh Al, let the boy be"
I w-will not eat t-them

It was the same every week, usually about this time, Terry, without knocking, would breeze through our kitchen and into the living room where he would plop himself down in front of the Sylvania TV as the 1812 Overture began. We would hear Terry holler, "Hi, ho, Silver, away!" It was only many years later that I realized how important that cowboy mass

was for both Terry and me. For Terry, it was another ritual in a life full of rituals. They gave meaning to things which otherwise might seem trivial. I now see the triviality was mine, not Terry's. At that time, though, Terry's interruption was only a respite from my family's kitchen drama and from my stuttering.

Time has passed, and I grew out of that world, leaving it all behind. I saw Terry once more before he died. He remembered Dickie but had forgotten me. I remember him now with a sadness for things left unsaid. I now know how he blessed my existence through his own. Terry, I am now *kneeling* to say to you;

Benedict Vos,
Omnipatous deus pater
Et filius,
Et spiritus Sanctus.
Amen

Guns and Cigars

The photograph takes me back, and I smell gunpowder. The corn is dry, with pollen shaking itself off the tall stalks. We trample our way down separate rows of corn and weeds. The soil under our feet is upturned and alternately wet or dry, as if by chance. We stumble on clumps of earth placed in our paths, as if tormenting us. My cousins and I were maybe ten or eleven years old; it is hard to recall exactly, but it was the same every year.

Looking again at the old photograph, I see the men gathered around old Packards and Fords, with dead birds laid on the ground around them. The men are dressed for the hunt, my father looking a lot like F. Scott Fitzgerald with his pants legs tucked into tall leather boots, laced to the top. He looked urbane, even in the rough outdoors. All the men wore big hunting jackets with pockets and pouches for the shells and the birds to be bagged. The shotguns would come out of their cases with a rasping sound of bolts and slides. It seemed unnatural that metal could work upon metal in such smooth and deadly harmony. It was, for me, both terrifying and fascinating.

My uncles were World War II vets and looked dangerous standing there with their guns held loosely—like the cigars in their mouths. Their fathers, the ancient ones, seemed to be from another time and place too distant for me to admire. I do remember the bibbed overalls and big hands; foreign hands with ugly calluses and yellow/brown tobacco stains—hands fiddling with pocket watches and holding big cigars chewed to the nub. I can see the spittle as it sticks to their beards and stains on their shirt fronts. I see great uncle Rudy, with his cigar moving side to side as if pointing the way for his hunting dog. The dog was new and excitable, flushing birds well out of our range. "Goddamn dog." I still see the cigar twitching in anger and frustration.

It was the fifties, and we hunted out in western Minnesota on the Walstad farm owned by John and Ella. They were Norwegians of the old country. Often, I would hear them lapse into their native tongue. It sounded to me like the clucking of chickens. Everything seems like a clique to me now. John was taciturn and rarely spoke. Ella was in constant movement and rarely stopped talking. The farmhouse was old and smelled of cigars and Limburger cheese. Everything looked staged, with spittoons and tower ashtrays by every chair. On the wall, there was a large cardboard box which opened in sections to little red and green elves. The kitchen was huge, with room for all of us, and still able to contain Ella and Lena bustling about.

Lena was Ella's sister and lived with them. It seems appropriate now that she was a deaf-mute. She always seemed to hang around the edges, almost in hiding—like the birds we were going after. Many years later, I heard a rumor that she was the product of rape or incest. I don't know if this was true or not. Skeletons always seem to add flesh as they come out of the closet. Maybe, though, that is why she seemed to remind me of the capons we would eat on Saturday night. It was a special tradition; we would feast on capons while hunting pheasants.

As kids, we would stand around expectantly while one of the old men would chop the heads off the chickens, with us chasing the headless birds around the yard. I now know where I got the phrase, "You guys are running around like chickens with their heads cut off." My kids never got that from a vicarious level, so I was forced to change it to, "You guys look like a Chinese fire drill." This may be equally obscure, but they seem to dislike it better. Regardless, I remember blood spraying everywhere, splattering and staining our clothes, and we were proud of it.

Like I was proud when our fathers would play football with us in the yard. They would muscle and shove us around. Like dogs, we would always bounce back. They always seemed to quit, just as we got the upper hand. Football was a big part of the weekend; we picked numbers for the Gopher game. The pot often ran $30 or $40. I wanted that money. In the morning, we organized the hunt. We boys would serve as flushers, walking alongside the men. The old ones were sent ahead to the end of the field or slough. I thought it was in deference to their age or frailty. I was wrong and quickly learned they were the *crack shots* and were placed there to get the birds we flushed too soon or missed.

One year (I don't remember which one), we got our own guns. Mine was a J. C. Higgins 20-gauge bolt action, with a clip. I wanted to load the clip, but my father would not let me. "You only get one shot. If you miss, you're too late anyway." I am not sure he was right, but the words stuck. I remember the first pheasant I killed. We were in a slough, mud up past my ankles. It is cold and miserable; suddenly, a cock flew up. *Whoosh! Flap flap flap.* Scared out of my wits, I shoot quickly just as it rises over my head. Even today, I tell my boys, "You got to take aim and strike quickly before the opportunity passes." I doubt if they believe me, nothing is a single shot anymore. "Good shot. Go get it." Quickly, I fetched the bird and gave it the *coup de grâce* by grabbing the neck and twirling it around my head. God, it was so beautiful, the red neck and long feathers like a badge of honor for both of us. I wanted to hold it forever, like the ones in the photo.

After the hunt, we would sneak off for Camels or Lucky Strikes. Although I am sure the men knew what we were up to, they tolerated our little game. The day had cleared up beautifully, geese were everywhere. Flocks of them would land, but we never hunted them. It was like they were sacred, even for the men. Once we saw a white snow goose land, and we all stopped to admire its specialness. The goose was going on a journey of thousands of miles to places we could not yet imagine. We all knew it was not our place to disturb its freedom to pass us by.

At night, my uncle, who had been an infantry sergeant (a lot like Vic Morrow in the old TV show, *Combat*), would tell us stories of Japs and turkey shoots. We listened intently as he told us of prisoners they would let go, only to run into an open field and certain death. It seemed wonderful to be able to kill Japs with such ease. He also told us of the joys of sex. We didn't know exactly what he was talking about but nodded appropriately and spit on the ground.

The world was simple then, and we were simple. We had no idea how complicated things would become. The men talked to each other, and we watched and listened. We listened and learned. Those times are gone now, along with the men. They died with tubes up their noses and fear in their eyes. I see the fear and want a good cigar but can't find one anywhere.

Exclusive Interview with God

Interviewer:
Welcome. I appreciate this opportunity.
What made you decide to talk now?

God:
Thank you. I appreciate this opportunity. I am always available. What made you decide to listen?

I mean, why today? Why me? Why this room?

Because you chose it and made it happen.

Are you the one and only God?

I am whatever you choose to call me.

Are you the Creator?

No more or less than you are.

Why is there so much evil, sickness, and death?

I created life in all its infiniteness and completeness. Evil, sickness, and death are human choices—not mine.

But death!

Death is only a word, not a state of not-being. Do you believe in religion?

I am not opposed to anything being created as a good. I imagined things might have turned out better, but I am sure so did you.

Could you make things better?

Yes, so can you.

Are there any people on Earth, living or dead, you admire?

Tough question. I have to say, all my children have souls I admire.

If so, how can you let the children suffer?

I don't let or want it to happen any more than you do. We allow it to happen. My power to change it is linked with you.

So, does your power have limits?

Only as far as your power is untapped.

Is there life after death and a resurrection or reincarnation?

Since I don't buy death, all the rest is irrelevant. Imagine a circle growing larger and larger, ever colliding and spinning. Imagine the energy created, flinging out what it has spun. Imagine all the circles connecting throughout infinity. Your scientists today are getting close to the nexus of what we call eternity.

Wow!
Why can't we remember the past or feel the future?

Because you choose not to.

Come on; that tells me nothing.

Okay, think of time and beliefs as limits, or
caps, man places on his abilities.

Like "The Little Engine That Could" or "High Hopes"?

No, simple positivism is linear and ignores the links circling us.

Yet, before, you described circles colliding and
connecting. Doesn't that imply a separateness?

Yes, separate in time but not in space.

Wow! Again. You are heavy. Can you make
a miracle now, this minute?

Yes.

Well?

Well, what?

Do it.

I did; you are talking to God, aren't you? Want another?
Think of someone you love. Imagine calling for them. They
will hear you. Call your son's son's son. He will hear you.

I meant a physical miracle, like the parting of the Red Sea.

You are alive, aren't you? Every day I replenish your
cells, process your food, give you pleasure, and
warn you of pain. What more do you want?

I want positive, verifiable proof that God
exists and can make things happen.

You are that proof. You can do anything but not alone.
I must leave now for a while.

Why?

Because I sense you are tired. I can feel
your energy and belief fading…

Glossing the Bible

The Good Corinthians

I am going to write to him about this whole situation. It has become intolerable. All I hear is about Paul's agape. One would think he is the Messiah, not Jesus. You women always take things too literally. It has been almost three years since his visit. The women still cluck and gaggle every time his name comes up. I am getting irritated with all their barnyard philosophy.

The foundation of Christianity, and our conversion, is rooted in the finest tradition of male philosophers. We have been schooled in this for centuries. The Roman and Hebrew heretics have failed to budge us from the masculine truth at its base. Why do they feel it necessary to peck and claw at these basic truisms? By Zeus, I am going to put an end to this right now. Your inept glossing of the word galls me as the man chosen by Paul to lead you. When Paul spoke of the separation of body and spirit, he did not mean from your husband. The husband is the master and ruler of his house. The only authority in marriage is through the husband. This is sacred in the eyes of God. Your duties and obligations as a wife are also sacred. You will obey your husband as you obey God. I am a Christian and therefore a patient and suffering man. I will write to you, Paul, and will await his answer before thrashing you.

Dear Paul,

> I greet you on behalf of your loyal and obedient children of Corinth. We have missed your teaching yet are blessed by your spiritual presence, through your disciple, Timothy. As the

leader of your young and growing church in our community, I send my humble blessings to you in the spirit of our Lord and Savior, Jesus Christ.

I write to you now as a suffering servant of your words, which have been abused and misused by some of your less knowledgeable converts. You and I know well that wisdom requires the fertilization of male logic. Only God and his agent, man, can plant the seeds of wisdom. There are some females in our flock who view Christianity as a garden, which will grow without reason. Others see it as a field, with men hitched to the plow, or apples ripe for the picking. Still, others see it as a desert—a barren monastery where no man can plant a seed.

When I quote the Bible, and your words, they toss their hair in blasphemy. One even had the gall to suggest celibacy was God's law. Using your name as an authority, another (proving her contradictory nature) even said God required her to go forth and multiply—often. Frankly, Paul, I am at my wit's end. How does one apply logic and argument to a sex devoid of these virtues? I ask, I pray, I beg you to please write to them; they need your special guidance and a firm hand. In the name of Zeus and Apollo and our Lord Jesus, I will pray each day for your words to help re-establish the proper order in our community.

As fathers of Christ's children, we share in the duty of guiding our sometimes silly, but always loving children. I remain armed in the silence of truth and shielded by my faith in you as a Man of God.

Your respectful servant, and a good Corinthian

A Good Corinthian Wife Responds

Thank the Lord he has settled down. The male is such a peacock. His feathers were ruffled for weeks awaiting Paul's response. As well as I know my husband, I know almost verbatim what he said to Paul. I love Paul, but I don't need his interpretation of words from the Messiah. He the Lord Jesus, understood us as outsiders. He was the blessed son of the Virgin Mary. He was the only man to touch the true soul of women. Yet even he dared not question the words of his Father, who told us to go forth and multiply. I have followed his Word literally and have given him eight children, added to our flock.

Paul, in his diplomatic way, supports all my arguments. My gift from God is blessed through marriage. I am free of the fires of sin. God commanded man to love and refresh us. Daughters, listen well. *Purity* and *virginity* are relative terms of little importance in the long-term view of life. The male in his frailty is closer to the end and hence his limited view of God's judgment.

I agree that men like Paul should be chaste in their nearness to heaven. We women are closer to the earth and are one with the cycle of birth and death. We do not need the links of logic nor the chains of authority to carry out God's will. Paul says we are mutually dependent. I would suggest he knows well the dependent nature of his sex. In fact, he commands us in the name of God to save man. Daughters, I leave you with Paul's commandment: we must help guide our husbands into heaven. It may be our purgatory, but suffering is second nature to us anyway.

From a good Corinthian woman

The Wall

We see them come and go, entering our silence with their busy thoughts, trying to fill a void in themselves through us. I see more approaching now with soft, reverent steps. I would guess they are businesspeople, from the suits and open trench coats. There are three of them; their energy seems separate and diffused. I must wait for them to focus. I know what will come, and my anticipation is—"Duncan, Dunn, Durant."

Where was I in '68? Honey was pregnant, and our marriage was still new and exciting. It was a long time ago. I'm getting wet and cold. I wish they would hurry. A drink sounds good right now. What are they thinking about? She couldn't have been five or six years old when Frank was there. He is the one I'm concerned about today. He never says anything at work, and I have learned not to ask. Peggy sure looks good; maybe it's just her youth. She is so small. I could lift her easily as we made love. Her boyfriend, Peter, is a jerk. Frank would be much better for her, if only he wasn't so… It's not guilt I feel now. I made my choices back in '62, well before the shit hit the fan.

There wasn't even a war back then. I enlisted in the Army Reserves as my best option. I was flunking college and didn't want to sit at home with all the criticisms. I spent six lousy years paying my dues. All I wanted was to get on with my life. The times were filled with conflict and contradictions. The country was advancing with leaps and bounds. Kids today cannot imagine the excitement of computers and the space program. It was amazing, even being on the periphery. I can only feel a distant sadness for all those boys I have missed. Peggy is kneeling and touching the black marble. Why? Does she believe it will answer? I'm hungry; tomorrow's going to be boring. They still believe meetings accomplish things. Frank and I know better; maybe he is ready to leave.

"Mack, Mallory, Marcino"

Sally told me he was nineteen years old in 1972, the same age as my brother Danny. The only memory I have of him is the book Sally showed me at school. Michael's page was full of boys with short haircuts and big ears. They all looked alike. I wonder what Michael's page would look like today. How many blank spots would there be? Here he is: Marcino, reduced to a name etched on a wall. A monument to minimalism. The reduction of the past as a service to the future. It makes me sick; Frank and Michael would have been about the same age then. I wonder how Frank is doing. It must be so hard for him. John looks uncomfortable, so old and sad. Maybe if I touch...

Peter told me he was exempt from the draft because he had tripped on the steps getting into a Freedom Bus. Whenever he talks about those days, I can sense his excitement and restlessness. Maybe that's part of our problem. I cannot match up to his memories. Is that my fault? I do want a home and children. Is that a crime?

I can feel Peter's fear of the future. What is he afraid of? I bet Michael would trade places with him. I get so mad at Peter sometimes. He calls John and Frank the *bore brothers*. He says they are kindred spirits of the inane. If living today is such a bore, maybe he would like to trade places—what do you think of that, Michael?

"Schnider, Schoner, Sholl."

You jerk. We had it made. All we had to do was smoke a little grass and lay low. But you had to go out there and see what was going on. I believe it was the music that drove you out. Mick Jagger put you on this wall. I'll never forgive The Stones for that. The statue over there is a goddamn farce. Yuppie soldiers in bronze standing and holding their M14s like goddamn briefcases. We survived over a year by not standing up for anything. How many times have we talked of the odds? Why didn't you listen? You died for, and by, the good old US Army. Did our colonel add you to the weekly KIAs?

Do you care? I cared then, but I don't anymore. I came to tell you that you did beat the odds in the long run. You haven't missed much. Want to hear a good joke? The company I work for is paying me to design systems that will defend us from missiles launched from outer space. Hah; we couldn't find the "gooks" from twenty feet away, and now we are going to stop the Russians from twenty thousand miles up—give me a break! John, are you ready to go? Karl, I wanted to see you, but I must say you disappointed me. You have faded too much. I loved you once, I did…

They come, and they go, only a few suspect we are waiting. Energy and mass are part of a continuum. We feed on them and are mutually dependent—separated only by a thin wall that some call memory and their reality.

Three Little Maggots

A maggot is the larval stage of a winged creature. An obsolete sense of the word is a whimsical entertainment or dance.

—From *A Maggot*, John Fowles

Verse 1

The Manifesto

Men, let's unite
Come join me in the fight
To take back our God-given right
To ignore their hurts and slights

Our battle is just
God gave us the lust,
To sit and paw in the dust
And live without fear or trust
Men, aren't you tired of
Stories of their plight
To fit into their tights
Their daily fears and frights
And how lonely are their nights

Listen to me, and I'll make you free
To ignore their constant pleas
And their never-ending need
To plant discordant seeds, and to constantly tease

Would John Wayne dialogue?
Would Bogart relate?
Could Rhett Butler adjust?
Or would Cagney hesitate?

Doris Day, we miss you
Where are the Peggy Lees?
What happened to Cher?
Is she happy and free

Marilyn, you betrayed us
You knew sports and literature don't mix
Your life became a drama
Even DiMaggio couldn't fix

What happened to Ozzie
You couldn't show Ricky the way
And Mr. Cleaver how could you let
Beaver get fat and allow Wally to go gray

Now Loren Greene does dog commercials
And Michael Landon wears wings
Lloyd Nolan sells insurance
And Clint Eastwood sings

What's the world coming to
What is a real man to do
Take back our rightful place, to rule as before
And to control everything with humility and grace

Verse II

On the Arts

Trying to remember all
The authors from my past
Trying to recreate, and
To bring them all back

Shakespeare, Dickens, Dreiser
Tolstoy, Melville, Crane
Fitzgerald, Hemingway, Stendhal
Writers of great fame

Whitman, Cummings, Yeats
Eliot, Frost, Poe
Longfellow, Thomas, Dickenson
Poets from long ago

Jesus! I've loved them all
Hammett, Halprin, Hesse
I still see Rhett and Scarlett
And want to fix their mess

God! To make a character
And a story comes alive
Can't think of anything better
To do before I die

I remember Lawrence's women
As if they were my own
I still smell the flowers
In a verse from a Heine poem

Ah! And Dickens, the Scrooge, and the Twist
A Tale of Two Cities
With great plots and wit

The *hands* of Sherwood Anderson
I still feel their touch today
And even Wambaugh could paint
An onion field of gray

Fitzgerald and Hemingway pictured
A time and places, I'll never know
And Walt Whitman encapsulated
All of life in a poem

To create a story and to draw you in
Like Tolstoy and Poe
To open a window to adventure
Like Dumas and Hugo

Now don't get me wrong
I love the visual arts
In fact, on a cultural basis
TV and movies play a huge part

Star Trek and the Westerns
Gunsmoke and all the rest
Mary, Lou, and Ted were just a few of the best

But when you look carefully
And pull back from the set
Captain Kirk and Mr. Spock
Were only Bradbury's second best

And Matt Dillon is Rhett Butler
Neutered for TV
And Gleason's *The Honeymooners*
Are Shakespeare acting the rube

Now I know TV's getting hotter
And thank you, I'd like to say
Can't wait to see Lady Chatterley
Played by Doris Day

What I really think should happen, CBS could lead the way
Maybe do Proust's *Remembrance*
As a twenty-six-part play

In competition for ratings
NBC could do Moby Dick
With Curt Gowdy as Ahab
And as Ishmael, Bubba Smith

For ABC, I think Don Quixote
With Steve Martin in the title role
Sancho could be Woody Allen
And for villains, Three Dog Night

Now for the movies
I can't leave them out
They gave us *Citizen Kane*
And *Bonzo's Night Out*

Since movies today are torrid
Dante's *Inferno* should be filmed
With Madonna as a vestal virgin
And as the gatekeeper, Sean Penn

With all the vices captured
They would draw a massive crowd
The music score—unearthly
Twisted Sister wearing shrouds

Donna Rice and Jessica Hahn
Could be bit players on their way
Bakker, Falwell, and Robertson
Evangelists in the fray

Heston could replay *Moses*
Burt Lancaster, Elmer Gantry
Meryl Streep as Golda Meir
And Dustin Hoffman as Gandhi

The epic would summarize
All the films of the past
Codirected by Brooks and Allen
Who could ask for anything more

To make people real, and
Bring their thoughts alive
Isn't that the reason why
We watch and we cry

When Sophie made her choice
If you felt a part of her pain
Then both the book and the movie
Were a success, and not a game

Maybe it's appropriate today
All the media have mixed
Since Ronnie's in the White House
And Ollie North is playing politics

It shames me to think
That in a thousand years
Someone sifting through the rubble
Might think *American Idol* brought us near

From our movies and our books
They might think us masochists
Ruled by whims and fantasies
And generally, very sick

If the media's the message, they are carrying a woeful tune
Of a mixed and greedy people
Racing toward their doom

Yet they would also see redemption
Buried among the trash
Would appreciate all the connections
That we have kept with our past

You choose what to watch or read
You choose what to share
You select your reality
God, and I, don't care

Verse III

A Revelation

Like from a dream slowly waking, I crossed the room shaking. I felt a presence, silent yet oppressive, whispering, "I don't care."

As if given the gift of tongues, words filled my lungs. Babble from every age, words filled with rage. I felt the pain of billions calling his name. Ageless questions filled the night, but the answers took flight. Crying, I was lifted. I knew I must be dead. Transported up and away, I thought this must be my day. Floating always upward, things turned bright and clear. Memories unfolded; I knew I must be nearby. A breeze took the clouds away. I opened my eyes to see. Finally, to get the answers, to how I wanted things to be. I saw Bud and Lou approaching, a lineup in their hands, and knowing a cosmic joke when I saw one, I thought, where's the Brass Band? Smiling to show my wit, thinking I would play their game, I asked, "Who's in charge? What is his name?" They wept and replied, "We don't know."

I suddenly felt a poke and awoke. She asked about my dream. I said, "Not a dream, a nightmare." She asked, "What do you mean?" "It's better not to know about yesterday and tomorrow
And who's on first, and
What's his name."
She said, "What are you talking about?"
I replied, "I don't know."

Reflections in a Mirror

A Song/Poem

Richard Dean Holmberg

Almost suspended, we are laid asleep in body, and
Become a living soul and while we with an eye
Made quiet by their power of harmony, and the
Deep power of joy, we see into the life of things

—William Wordsworth
From "The Prelude"

Reflections in a mirror
Discoveries of oneself
Reflections in a mirror
Revealing a hidden wealth

Encounter with oneself
Is more than looking in a mirror
It's reaching out to others
And sharing all our fears

Verse 1
Discovery of feelings
Buried deep withins
Discovery of Love and sharing,
And wondering where I've been
Looking to tomorrow
With anticipation and joy

Looking to tomorrow the
Wonders to employ
Asking questions of life
The God who wasn't there
Asking questions as to why
My soul was not aware
Aware of the feelings, and
The many things we share
Aware of the opportunity
Given us to care

CHORUS

VERSE 2
I know that I've been changed
But I don't know quite how
I know I've been joined
Together with a crowd
A crowd that's building slowly
From the bottom to the top
A crowd planting seeds of love
And yielding a bountiful crop
The promise of tomorrow
A gift of a God who cares.
The promise of a power
Which all of us can share

REPEAT CHORUS

VERSE 3
It's the giving and receiving
Of all that life can bring
Is a song of love together
The golden circle of a ring
If you don't believe me
Just look into your mirror

Remove the masks, release the shame
And let go of all your fears
What you will see is the glory
Missing all these years
The beginning of our story of love without the tears

Chorus

Encounter

I wake to sleep and take my waking slow.
Learn by going where I have to go…

—T. Roethke

Lessons

I have carried some demons inside me
And they have refused to let me go
With them, I have never been free
My life a picture show.

They were pride, ego, and selfishness
I was smarter than all the rest
Dependent on no one
My life is an awful mess.

Nothing was needed, and
Nothing was given
Feelings a weakness
Not shown, but hidden

I didn't believe in God
Or *if* I did
Felt him irrelevant
Laughed at him, a
He taught me a lesson

He released the demons
Let me have my way
Together they rode rampant
Eventually winning the day

They took over and haunted me
Ran me around in circles
Look at all the havoc
That they wrought on me

I've learned that I hurt
And must share feelings
I've learned that I must return
All the good I've been receiving

To be aware of what I have to offer
And to be willing to pass it through
Will provide me with the reason
To keep on loving you

Over the Rainbow

Something will come of this
Of that, I am assured
Something good will happen
There must be a cure
The sickness is in our culture
Infecting my soul
I'm dying of a morality
Irrelevant, I'm told
It is more than aids or cancer
It's a kind of fatal apathy
With God who set us free
The dead father has led us
Nowhere, on a rudderless ship
Sailing into capricious winds
Under merciless mental whips
Civility and education only hide
The portrait of Dorian Gray
Behind the mirror and makeup
We are all molded in clay
Science has become revisionist
Business still a vicious game
Politics and law; travesties
Religion a battle of names

Our foundations are sandcastles
And mud puddles of myths
That we are all *okay*
A psychological last ditch

So round them up,
And bring them all around
Both the good and the bad
I'm here to tell a tale
That's sad, sad, sad
Now listen up and listen tight
You've got to change your ways
The times a coming soon partner
On that great reckoning day

You have got to take a stand
Line up on a side
The alternative is nothing
Nothing but suicide

It's not glory, truth, or honor
Deeds will not save the day
Reason is not the answer,
And chance the only way

How many tears must fall
Before we are allowed to see
The God who made us human
And who wants us to be free

Something good must happen
That's what it's all about
There's an order in the chaos
Our questions can't bring out

Something good is coming
I can see it just ahead
Something good will happen if I can just
Remove this dread

Purge

Advice and counsel
Screwing with my mind
Friends and colleagues
Trying to be kind

Metaphysics or meditation
Don't lessen the fear
Intellectual awareness
Won't bring me near

My body's hurting
My head's a mess
All I want is to
Avoid these tests

Don't need an Audi
Don't want no fame
Can't reconcile the feeling
It's all a rigged game

My body's sending signals
Responding to the pain
The transformation's frightening
Everything's going lame

I cannot celebrate myself
Cannot sing a song
I don't understand who
Is right, and what is wrong

I keep thinking of income
Debt, and cash flow
I keep thinking of us
And how we are on hold

I want to feel the passion, and
I thirst for the grape
But I can't shake the feeling
That maybe we have been raped

Or maybe we have taken each other
From some past life, where we met
And somehow in this time
We are repaying a karmic debt

I used to be so sure
Banked on integrity and wit
Now I'm starting to locate
All the leaks in my ship

My excuse was naivety
A "barefoot boy with cheek"
My response was not humorous
But self-deprecating and weak

If the body is a reflection
Of what is going on inside
I better get a checkup
And better find out why

My batteries are running low
My radiator's sprung a leak
I feel like an Edsel
And look like a jeep

My front end's shaking
And the rear's not too sound
Running down the highway
Don't know what road I am on

It is okay, I like to travel
I've always driven fast
The problem is not being sure of
Where I am headed, or the way back

You see, I'm over forty and
Have studied cause and effect
That is why I am worried
I will end up a bloody wreck

A Memory

Traveling back in time
Remembering things unkind
Dredging up the past
The memories come back

I see a boy in tears
Rocking, rocking the years
Stammering, stuttering through life
Avoiding conflict and strife

Thoughts come back, as
Lights through a crack
Rocking, rocking to sleep
His childhood to keep

Grown up now, gone away
The crutches of the past
Lingering, still the same
Chewed-up nails and pain

A Rebirthing

He walked out the door
And drove quickly away
Left everything behind
Had nothing to say
And nowhere to go
So he just went away

He had no plans
No axes to grind
He was a simple man
Who got left behind

He wanted to feel
Too much, and more
Soon everything real
Became a trial, and a bore

He was half here, and half there
Away in the past
Walt would understand
How he felt so small
And so vast

He wept for the universe
For a billion dead stars

But could not distinguish
The close from the far

He needs to be reborn
To rebuild his heart and soul
He needs a reason for living
Without conditions and control

He can't go halfway
It is either here or there
He can't block the love
That tells him we care, and
Requires him to share

November '82

Bright morning, white light
Everything crystal clear
Why didn't we know of
The changes so near?

It comes so quickly
God, what a sight
Changing the seasons
Deep in the night

Winter with its bitter cold
Clean, clear, and white
Rushes in quickly
On the winds of fright

Chilling us to the bones
Frost is in the air
Ice, as a warning
Telling us to prepare

Bundle up with blankets
Crawl deep into the bed
Hide under the covers
You know what is ahead

The signs are evident
Before you retire
We sleep through the night
Unaware of what has transpired

The changes will come
We don't have a say
We are not in charge, and
Don't know the way

They come with the seasons
And grow with our fears
Exist in the cold
See them coming near

Since we believe in the seasons
And the changes brought about
Aren't we a little foolish
To live our lives in doubt?

Change

And the kelson of creation is love…
All forces have been steadily employed
To complete and delight me
Now on this spot
I stand with my robust soul…

—Walt Whitman

With Regrets, I Say Goodbye

Death caught you on the fly
With no time for goodbyes
I'll never know why
You had to die
And I can't cry

I walked through the days
Following your death
Not thinking of you
Finding else to do

Once in a while, it hurt
When I opened my heart
A memory would flash by
A tear would start and die

My excuse was with the living
Grief could come much later
But time passed you by
And it's too late to cry

Sometimes I wonder why
You and I grew apart so late
I didn't hear your caring
We missed our time for sharing

Thinking of you, I think of mine
The flaw is in our likeness
I'm guilty of what they're missing
Giving love is more than wishing

Maybe love and guilt go together
Like good and bad weather
Passing from father to son
Regretting what is left undone

I know that I loved you
And that you loved me
Each in our silent way
Never knew what or how to say

You didn't say why
And I couldn't say goodbye
The words wouldn't come
Until it was all done
And time passed us by

An Apology from My Soul

How can I write
What I do not know
How can the pen flow
From a barren soul.
I don't know what it's all about
But somehow the words
Just want to shout
The feelings come
Without any help
The words seem to fall
From an empty shelf
The words keep coming from somewhere within
Revealing all my hidden sins
But I don't feel any pain
Maybe I can write
Without any shame
The pen that moves
And calls your name
Must somehow take
All the blame
I am not responsible
For what you write
I usually try
To keep it light
But you won't let me
Forget my doubts
You seem to know
What it's all about
So I'll reconcile
And go it your way

Let you speak
And have your way
Until the time when I will find
Your words reflect
What's on my mind.

A Walk in the Park

(for June and Paul)

One day as I was walking
Strolling down a path
Contemplating tragedy and
All of life's lack
Burdened with sad memories
Failures and shame
Humbled by a feeling
That nothing can change
With head bent downward
Afraid to face the sky
Daring not to look ahead
Too frightened to ask why
Stumbling on a rock
Which fate put in my way
They took my hand and led me
To a place in the shade
Numbed with fear I followed
Not wanting to see the trees
Dumb with thoughts I listened
To the wind blowing free
The old man and woman beckoned
"Come join us on the heights"
Whispering words of wisdom
I said, "Let me be
Let me be"
Sitting, we held hands
And they encouraged me to see
A world full of choices

It's up to me
It's up to me
They asked me to look up
Though I preferred to look down
Saw visions and possibilities
To be free
To be free
Floating away I saw them
Still sitting by the tree
Silently I waved thanks
For allowing me
To be me
To be me.

Christmas '87

I have given many presents
And received many more
This Christmas is very special
A gifting of my soul
I can say, "Merry Christmas"
Have a joyful '88
Let's bring love and peace
And purge the world of hate

But who am I to lecture
How can I advise
What can I tell you
That's not a compromise

We live with reservations
And witness senseless hate
We all want to change things
Then we wait, or hesitate

We look for doors to reason
We search out paths to love
And we all want soulmates
And guidance from above

I know what I speak
Been down this road before
Looking for all the answers
And waiting to be told

It seems I always find
A locked fence or gate
It seems a part of me
Always must wait

Maybe I agree with Holly
Though that's hard to admit
The answers to knowing
To ourselves we must commit

I am not spiritual
But agree I must go inside
To find a God who loves us
And is our mentor and guide

A gathering like tonight
A meeting of kindred souls
An abundance of energy is present
A kind of metaphysical "black hole"

The power joined is electrical
We are in the eye of the storm
Tonight is a special opportunity
To share in a communal warm

So my Christmas gift to you
Is to tap into the spark and,
Splicing with the energy
Absorbing love along the arc

Heaven's Gate

Out from the earth, and
Moving among the stars
The dream became real,
Of what once seemed so far

Merging into the trees
Looking out across the night
Quietly absorbing the beauty
Of nature with wonder and delight

The lake below was crystal clear
Like nothing I've seen before
The loons were swimming softly
Softly along the shore

My gun and I were comfortable
As if I was part of the land
Faded memories of past hunts
As we sat there hand in hand

We were looking for the beavers
Who had ravaged my trees
Biological determinism be damned
Hot lead was their destiny

An eagle landed on my left looking curiously at me
Destroyer, interloper, or owner
What is your need?

The cabin was on my right
Standing alone on a point
A church among the pines
Which no man could anoint

At dusk, in silent tandem
They came—U-boats in the night
Ready to torpedo my timbers
By God, not tonight

Almost too dark to see the varmints
I tracked them by their wakes
Knew they were armed and dangerous
Ready to prowl my lake

Then one turned toward shore
And I prepared for the kill
Somehow, he sensed my bloodlust
And retreated before my will

The victory was, at best, a stalemate
There was a little give-and-take
It was a minor compromise
Between me, them, and the lake

The metaphor of battle
Win lose, or balance of power
Was what I was taught about life
To fight, never to cower

So the beavers get a few trees
What's it to me?
I will fall asleep tonight
Reaming of eternity

The cabin is allegorical
A waystation to the stars
A place of birth and renewal
Before I travel afar

Heaven's gate is a meeting place
A land of trees and dreams
A sanctuary of spiritual freedom
On a lake of empathy

I am not the guardian nor
A keeper of the gate
I'm simply a lonely sentinel
To keep out fear and hate

For My Wife

Holly, it is you I praise
Looking back upon the years
The love you fed and nurtured
Despite all our fears
Though our marriage was expedient
A simple, mindless entry
You found a way through the seasons
To give our lives a reason
The pressures you faced in discovering
The validity of your identity
Give a witness to your ability
To cope with any adversity
The tug and pull of loyalties'
Father/mother/husband new
With the seed of responsibility
Planted in your womb.
Holly, it is you I praise
Your reaching, touching ways
My song is one of thankfulness
A gift for you today
Your soul is like a seed
Planted in the ground
Growing and developing
With people all around
Your understanding tenderness
In the face of thoughtlessness
Is not from simplemindedness
But from a god given openness
Holly, it is you I praise on this our special day let our song go on in
Harmony as the years pass away

Gatherings

Gatherings

The Drummer Boy

Ah listen,
Ah listen,
To the beat, the rhythm of the drums

The sounds of a hundred horses
The yells of a thousand men
The rumble of the cannon
The rifles firing minié balls

But look, it's a drummer boy
A mere child, beating, beating
The rhythm of a mighty band.

The battle is over
The winner and loser have left
Leaving behind the drummer boy
To carry on the chorus of death.

1956

The Desk

The years are hidden somewhere
Carefully documented, with layers
And layers of typed memos filed
Away neatly and submerged
Within those metal drawers.

It is my kingdom and my prison
Every thought and action
Limited by their dimensions
I cling to them as to a mistress
Knowing every shape, curve, and angle
Of those metal drawers

If it was up to me, I'd leave my desk
Roam the fields, and dance a jig
wear A wig and write a book
Or buy a boat and float
To the land of my dreams
But my desk is locked up tight
And I have lost the keys
Dead storing freedom and
Filing away eternity

1966

Daydreams

It was here in Minnesota
As I sat away the day
Looking through plate glass windows
At things across the way
The office was built for comfort
Decorous, modern too
Outside the earth grew colors
The sky was like a pool
For autumn in the northland
Is really, very grand
The crowning achievement
Of some carefully conceived plan
It's as if God was in a hurry
Before the winter cold
Sweeping multicolored brushstrokes
Like a painter extra bold
Would it be a crime or some form of treason
For me to go out and enjoy
This beautiful season
To put away my work
And walk among the trees
Although by the wall clock
It's not even three
I will not leave my desk
And I will take all the calls
I will not stop my labors
Except to roam the halls

That doesn't mean that isn't fun
To play with time this way
By scribbling rhymes and relaxing
On this fine autumn day

1974

Wonderrama

(An old TV show)

When I was a child like you
A very short time ago
I thought of all the things I'd do
If only I were old
I'd rule my home
As lord master and king
Take orders from no one
And do any old thing
I'd visit the zoo
Swim in a pool
Win every fight and
Stay up all night
Eat cookies for breakfast
Drink pop for lunch
Make popcorn for supper
And have a midnight brunch
Now that I'm older and the father of three
I don't need these things
The best I have is free
Your special to look at
And wonderful to hold
A reflection of everything
Sassy and bold
You're a challenge to my senses
Asking questions in numbers untold
I dread the day I'll have to let go
So if I forget as
I've been known to do

Remind me of this song
That was written for you.
Kids are people too
Wack-a-do, wack-a-do

1977

Winning

(For my boys)

What a boon to gain the game
To strive and achieve glory and fame
To be at the top of the athletic mainstream
To reach out and grab the American dream
Lombardi said, "Everything it isn't
Winning is the only thing. Is it?"
Now everyone gathers to see a fine catch
And to shout obscenities, and scream at the ref
In the game of hockey
To fight is honorable and right
To crosscheck and maybe break a bone
And to cut up the losers before going home
To compete in the ring is allegros to life
As Nixon can bear witness, or maybe his wife
The thrill of victory the agony of defeat
If winning is so important, why not cheat
When boys are little, they dream the dreams
Of trophies, scholarships, and being on the team
It's of sports and politics, and life that I speak
The goal of goals is at its peak
What should I say to my sons who are young
That someday you can be number one
Or should I say young man do not fear
For winning or losing you'll always be dear.

1980

All God's Children

They come from heaven
They do, they do
Given to us
Through you, through you
We are lucky
Don't you know giving us love
As they unfold
And spreading joy as
They blossom and grow
Who can know where they will go
Do we really want to know
Can we protect them from our pasts
Will any of our teachings really last
Each must learn and live and grow
Each a separate story told
They gain from us but
Return much more
And are always welcome at my door
I thank you, Lord
I do, I do
Will return them finally,
To you, to you.

1982

Prayer

I pray for you
And you for me
Together we are
Calling for thee
Hear us now
Hear our call
People listen
One and all
We're asking you
To join us now
Hear us and
We will show you how
To speak to God
And what to say
To prove to him
We have found the way
Not to beg
For his help
But to share
In his wealth
It will be given
If you believe
In the miracles that
Our prayers conceive

1982

ENIAC

I made a list of things today
Things that I would change
Put them with my other lists
To shuffle and rearrange
Each day I review the lists I've made
From the previous couple of days
Delete the ones I haven't done
And save for another day
It's been my lifelong habit
I'm good at making lists
Someday I'll buy an IBM
A dream I have often wished
I will database all my flaws
Pie chart all my fears
Calculate in binary terms
The value of my years, I've heard that heaven's going online
So I better set up backup files
To bring along at sign-off time

1986

On "Purple Rain"

A prince from the suburbs
Dressed in purple tights
Brought forth visions of
Dark and musical nights
Evoking good memories
Of women from the past
Fulfilling wishes of
"Nicki" on her back
Taunt little singer/poet
Prances and brays
Discordant guitar riffs
Showing me the way
"U" are black and
"I" white
"U" hot
"I" not
"U" may think I am crazy
But I'll not be satisfied
Until I know the reason
Why, "I would die for 'U'"
You took my thoughts
And lit them on fire
Rocking and dancing
Round a funeral pyre
Resurrected I ascended
Sharing a purple scorn
Writing of my father

Burdens unborn
I know we share nothing
But a common backyard
Black prince white bard

1987

General Ledger

Measuring life, by
Drips and drops
Of time
Spent

Memories, cashed in
Diminishing
Credit for
Tomorrow

Making a balance book
Of red and black
To someday
Reconcile

Mounds of ledger
Drawn up
Identifying
Unresolved differences
To be
Charged off
In the end

1987

About the Author

Richard Dean Holmberg retired when he turned eighty years old. He spent the previous thirty years in customer service, both in bookselling and retail, and credits this time to interacting and observing customers of all ages and interests. These interactions have kept him young at heart.